THE FURRY
MACCALOO

— Gillian Cross —

Illustrated by
MADELEINE BAKER

HEINEMANN · LONDON

First published in Great Britain 1993
by William Heinemann Ltd
an imprint of Reed Consumer Books Ltd
Michelin House
81 Fulham Road
London SW3 6RB

AUCKLAND · MELBOURNE · SINGAPORE · TORONTO

Printed in Italy by Olivotto

A school pack of BANANA BOOKS 55–60 is
available from Heinemann Educational Books
ISBN 0 435 00109 4

The Blue Bead

IT ALL BEGAN when Surinder borrowed
the beads. And that was Erica's fault.

Surinder and Julia were best friends
until Erica came to the school. Now
Erica wanted to be Julia's friend. The
two of them were always whispering
secrets, and if Surinder tried to join in,
Erica yelled: 'Go away, snoopy
Surinder! We've got a secret. We don't
want you.'

1

It was the same every day, and Surinder had no one to play with.

That was why she borrowed her mother's bead jar. It was just the right size to slip into her coat pocket. Next playtime, instead of following Julia and Erica, she knelt in a corner of the playground and tipped the beads into her lap.

Red and green and yellow ones.

Wooden globes, golden flowers and pottery chunks. And, right at the bottom, an oval one made of cloudy blue glass that caught the light as Surinder picked it up.

But not for long. There was a loud whoop. 'What are you doing, snoopy Surinder?'

Erica charged up, dragging Julia after her, and pushed Surinder over. The beads rolled into a puddle and Surinder grabbed at them.

'*Yuck*!' said Erica. 'Surinder's in the mud.'

'Surinder!' Mr Webster strode across the playground. 'You'll get filthy.'

'But Erica knocked my beads over.'

'No tales. Go in and wash your hands.'

Miserably, Surinder scooped the rest of the beads into the jar. They were dull and dirty now and they felt horrible.

She went inside and ran a basin of hot water. Then she tipped the beads in and swished them about. The cloudy blue bead was on top and she began to rub it clean.

FIZZ!!! A thin wisp of smoke curled over the basin.

'Ooh!' said a voice. 'I don't *like* it here!'

Sitting in the basin was a strange, furry animal, as big as a kitten. But it wasn't a kitten. It blinked unhappily at the white walls and bright, white basins.

Surinder gulped. 'W-where did you come from?'

'From a Delta-world, of course,' said the creature sulkily. 'I'm a Maccaloo, aren't I? And I was minding my own business in my nice, dark, *cosy* Delta-world. Why did you have to rub my

calling bead and bring me to this horrible *white* place?'

'This bead?' Surinder rubbed it again, and the Maccaloo shivered.

'Don't do that! It tickles. Get on with the wishes.'

'Wishes?' Surinder's eyes opened wide. 'Can you grant wishes?'

'Of course not!' said the Maccaloo. 'Don't you know anything? *You* have to grant *my* wishes.'

'*Me?*'

The Maccaloo sighed. 'You rubbed my calling bead. Now you have to grant me three wishes – or I can't go home.' It sniffed and a big, blue tear ran down its furry cheek.

'But I'm not magic,' Surinder said. 'I can't grant wishes.'

'You must. Or else I'll stay with you for ever. You can't get rid of me unless

you grant my wishes.' The Maccaloo
glared round at the basins and the white
walls. 'I wish . . .'

'It's no use,' said Surinder.

'. . . I wish . . .'

'I can't do magic!'

'I wish . . .' The Maccaloo raised its
voice. '. . . for NO WHITE! Anywhere
I look!' It beamed at Surinder. 'There
you are. That's an easy wish.'

'Easy?' Surinder said. 'Getting rid of

all the white in the world?'

'Simple,' said the Maccaloo. 'In a Delta-world, anyway.'

'Well, it's impossible here. Wish for something else.'

'But I can't.' The Maccaloo's bottom lip trembled. 'I've made my wish. And unless you grant it – *I can never go home*!'

It began to wail, and a stream of blue tears ran down its face and into the water.

'What's going on?' said a voice.

Surinder whirled round. Mrs Angus was in the doorway, staring suspiciously.

'I . . .' Surinder looked back at the basin, but the Maccaloo had gone. 'Mr Webster sent me in to wash my hands.'

'Well, hurry up. It's almost time for the bell.'

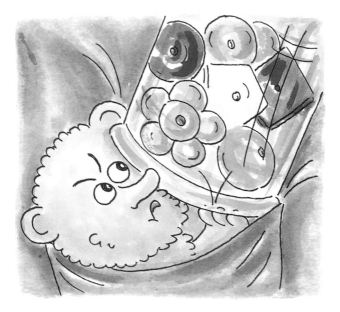

Mrs Angus strode off and Surinder
picked the beads out of the water and
dropped them into the jar. *Funny*, she
thought, *I must have imagined the
Maccaloo.* She put the lid on the jar and
dropped it into her pocket.

'OUCH!' said a cross voice.

The jar bounced up again and the
Maccaloo stuck its head out of the
pocket.

'You *thumped* me! And you *still* haven't granted my wish!'

'I can't grant it. Go away.'

Surinder grabbed the Maccaloo's shoulders and pulled, but it held fast to her pocket, and the lining began to rip.

Then the bell went.

'All right, stay there.' Surinder hung her coat on its peg, put the jar into the other pocket and picked up her bag.

But she hadn't got rid of the Maccaloo. As she walked into the classroom, someone tapped her arm.

'Hey! Your bag's wet.' It was David.

Erica was just behind. 'Look!' she yelled. 'Soggy old Surinder!'

Some people laughed, but David didn't. He looked at the damp patch. 'Is something leaking?'

'Don't know.' Surinder loosened the top cord. A wet, furry face peered up at her. And at the ceiling.

'White!' hissed the Maccaloo.

Surinder shut the bag quickly.

'OK?' said David.

Surinder's brain was buzzing. How could she get rid of the Maccaloo, before Erica found out?

'David . . .' It sounded silly, but she had to ask someone. 'How would you get rid of – white?'

David looked puzzled. 'White?'

'Yes. All the whiteness in the world.'

She was afraid he would laugh, but he didn't. He looked interested. 'I'll think about it.'

Surinder thought about it too. All day. Whenever she opened her bag, the Maccaloo stared miserably up at her. When she put her hand in, she felt wet fur, and once she was nipped by sharp little teeth.

Erica was watching. At hometime, she pounced on Surinder's bag.

'Let's see that!'

Grabbing the bag, she tossed it across the cloakroom to Julia and Julia threw it to Carl. David grabbed him and got the bag back.

'Thanks!' said Surinder.

But all the way home, she could hear the Maccaloo moaning softly. 'Oooh, I'm sore! I hate it here. Too white! I want to go home.'

No More White

THE MACCALOO SPENT the evening on Surinder's bed, sniffing miserably and nibbling a chapatti. She couldn't get rid of it.

All night she tossed and turned, wondering how she could grant its wish. Spray the school ceilings purple? Paint rainbows on the walls?

But that still left the clouds, and the

whites of people's eyes.

When she did sleep, she dreamed of green geese and bright yellow snow. And when she woke up the Maccaloo was under her pillow, whimpering and dropping blue tears on the sheet.

The next morning, when she walked
into school, David pushed something
into her hand and she stared stupidly at
it.

Two empty yellow toffee papers. The
kind you can see through.

'Well?' said David. 'You could make
frames for them. Like glasses.'

He took one back and held it up. And
then Surinder understood. His shirt
looked yellow. So did the whites of his
eyes. And the clouds behind his head.

'Brilliant!'

David grinned. 'Let's work together this morning. Then we can make the frames.'

'Great!' Surinder hid the sweet papers in her pocket, pretending not to see Erica and Julia staring at her.

She enjoyed working with David. They designed the best water-wheel in the class, and while David was testing it, Surinder cut some glasses from a scrap of card.

David frowned as he helped her glue the yellow sweet papers over the eyeholes. 'You've made them too small.'

'They're not for me,' Surinder said, without thinking. 'They're for the Macc . . .' She stopped.

'You don't have to tell me,' David said. 'Not if it's a secret.'

Surinder gulped. 'You won't tell Erica?'

'I won't tell anyone.'

'I'll show you at playtime then. Meet me behind the shed.'

The Second Wish

WHEN DAVID SAW the Maccaloo, he was astonished. He stood staring at it while Surinder explained.

'That's who the glasses are for?' he said.

Surinder nodded. 'Shut your eyes,' she said to the Maccaloo.

It wriggled in her arms. 'Why should I?'

'Shut your eyes!'

The Maccaloo threw a sorrowful look at David, to show how ill-used it was. Then it closed its eyes.

Surinder slipped on the glasses. 'There!'

The Maccaloo opened one eye. Then it opened the other. Then it opened both at once and stared across the playground.

'No white,' it whispered. 'No white.'
Grabbing one of Surinder's plaits, it
scrambled on to the top of her head.
'*My wish is granted*!' it yelled. 'Now I
wish . . .'

'Sssh!'

Surinder pulled it down and pushed it
into her pocket. Just in time. A second
later, Julia and Erica peered round the

shed.

Erica's eyes lit up. 'Look who's here! David and Surinder!' She pointed a finger at David. 'You *like* her!'

Julia giggled, and Surinder squirmed, but David just grinned.

'Of course I do. She's much nicer than you.'

'Huh!'

Erica flounced off, with Julia trailing behind, and David grinned again.

'That's settled her. Now where's the Maccaloo?'

It popped its head out of Surinder's pocket and beamed. 'I wish – for me to bounce,' it said happily.

'What?' David blinked.

The Maccaloo crawled up to Surinder's shoulder. It was dry now, and its fur was soft and warm. 'That's my second wish.'

Surinder groaned. 'You want to *bounce*?'

'It's easy.' The Maccaloo snuggled up to her cheek. 'Just give me Bouncing Medicine, or buy some Bouncing Socks.'

'We don't have Bouncing Medicine here,' Surinder said. 'Or Bouncing Socks. Why didn't you *ask*?'

'I thought I was *helping*.' The Maccaloo drooped. Blue tears splashed on to Surinder's blouse and she began to feel mean.

But David looked stern. 'Surinder's doing her best. Be nice to her!'

Sniffing, the Maccaloo dried its face on Surinder's cardigan. Then it curled up in her pocket. And Surinder spent the rest of the morning worrying about bouncing.

By dinnertime, she was desperate.

And so was the Maccaloo. It moaned hungrily in her bag. Surinder tried to save it some of her dinner, but she got scolded when Erica told Mr Webster.

Luckily, David had saved two sandwiches and a banana. They went behind the shed and the Maccaloo sat on Surinder's lap and munched while David drew plans for bouncing machines.

'We could tie balls to his feet. Or put him inside a football.'

'Hmm.' Surinder looked doubtfully at the sketches.

'Let's experiment,' David said eagerly. 'Come to tea tonight. And bring the Maccaloo.'

Surinder looked down at the small, furry bundle curled up in her lap. It had finished the food, and now it was snoring gently.

'Oh, the Maccaloo will come all right,' she said.

Bouncing

THE EXPERIMENTS WERE useless.

They cut open a football, but it just flopped around, with the Maccaloo inside, squealing angrily. And it squealed even louder when they tied balls to its feet.

'This world is horrible!' it snapped as its legs slid sideways. 'It should have Bouncing Socks.'

It sulked so much that, in the end, Surinder took it home. While she got ready for bed, it sat on her stool and grumbled.

'Do be quiet!' she said, as she undid her plaits. 'I'm thinking as hard as I can.'

The Maccaloo sniffed loudly, and she jumped. The elastic from her plait went twanging across the room.

'*That* can bounce,' the Maccaloo said crossly.

Surinder looked at the elastic. Then she grinned and picked it up. 'That's it, Maccaloo! You've found the answer!'

'I have?' said the Maccaloo.

'You'll see. Tomorrow. Now let me brush your fur.'

She brushed the Maccaloo until it was smooth and silky, and then let it snuggle into bed beside her. That night, they both slept soundly.

Boi-oi-oi-oi-oing!

ON THE WAY to school next morning,
Surinder bought three metres of strong
elastic. Erica and Julia saw her in the
shop, but she laughed and ran off before
they could find out what she'd bought.

David was waiting at the school gate,
with more plans for bouncing machines.
Surinder took out the elastic. 'How
about this? On the climbing frame?'

'But people will see,' said David.

'We'll do it during Assembly.'

When the class lined up to file into the Hall, Surinder and David slipped away to the climbing frame, by the back wall of the playground.

'Come on, Maccaloo,' said Surinder. 'You're going to bounce.'

The Maccaloo stuck its fluffy head suspiciously out of her pocket. 'How?'

'By elastic.' David pulled at the elastic, stretching it tight. Then he let it twang back. The Maccaloo blinked.

'Like *that*?'

'Exactly,' said David. 'With one end tied round you and the other one tied to the top of the climbing frame.'

'You'll go BOI-OI-OI-OI-OING!' said Surinder. She took the elastic and went up the climbing frame. The Maccaloo shuddered.

'High,' it whispered.

'You'll be quite safe.' Surinder tied a firm knot and let the rest of the elastic tumble down. 'David'll fix you on.'

The Maccaloo looked terrified. 'I'll bump into the ground.'

'No you won't,' said David. He lifted the Maccaloo up and made a loop round its waist. 'Look, the elastic doesn't reach the ground.'

'But it might break.'

'It's very strong,' said Surinder. 'Come on.'

Slowly, the Maccaloo started to climb. 'The knots might slip . . .'

When it reached her, Surinder tested all the knots. 'They're fine. Off you go!'

Very gently, she pushed the Maccaloo off the top bar of the climbing frame and it fell with a great wail.

But, a few centimetres above the
ground, it jerked to a stop. And bounced
up.

Then down again.

And up.

And down –

There was a long squeal of delight.

'I'm bouncing!'

'Sssh!' said Surinder. But it was too late.

'There they are!' yelled Erica, as the children poured out of school.

Hauling the Maccaloo to the top of the climbing frame, Surinder undid the knots as fast as she could. But Erica was almost there.

'They've got an animal! Let's catch it!'

The Maccaloo stared in terror. The moment it was free, it leapt out of

Surinder's arms, on to the wall. Then it disappeared over the top, into the park.

Surinder and David couldn't follow. Mrs Angus marched out and dragged them back into school. When Surinder tried to explain, she snorted.

'Don't give me fairy stories!'

She kept them in for the rest of the day. Surinder stared through the window, hoping the Maccaloo would come creeping across the playground, but there was no sign of it.

At hometime, she grabbed David. 'We've got to find it!'

He nodded, and they ran through the school gates and into the park. There was a tangle of trees and brambles against the school wall, and the ground underneath looked cold and damp.

'I'll start here,' Surinder said. 'You go up the other end.'

David ran off, and she started peering into the bushes. 'Maccaloo! Maccaloo, where are you?'

There was a whimper above her head. Looking up, she saw the Maccaloo shivering unhappily in the middle of a holly tree.

'Oh, you poor little thing!'

It leapt straight into her arms and she buttoned her coat round to keep it warm.

'David!'

He raced up, grinning. 'Wonderful! Only one more wish now. Then you can go home, Maccaloo.'

'Home!' The Maccaloo sniffed longingly as they walked out of the park. 'Oh, I wish . . .'

'Careful!' said Surinder.

'But I've had a brilliant idea.' The Maccaloo stuck its head out of her coat. 'I wish . . .'

'Wait!' said David.

The Maccaloo ignored him. 'I wish for whatever I'd like best in this world.'

'*What?*' said Surinder.

'That *is* impossible!' said David.

'Why?' The Maccaloo looked injured.

'You know what's in your world.'

'But there are *millions* of things.'
David said. 'It'll take us years to guess
what you'd like.'

The Maccaloo's eyes opened wide, but
before it could answer there was a shriek
from up the road.

'There they are!'

Erica and Julia were charging towards
them.

'Quick!' hissed David. 'My house!'

Surinder started to run, and the
Maccaloo bumped up and down inside
her coat.

'This is *horrible*!' it moaned. 'I want
to go home! *And never come to this
world again*!'

'But . . . you will . . .' Surinder
panted. 'If someone else . . . rubs the
bead you . . .'

Then she stopped dead. Suddenly she

knew. She *knew* how to grant the last
wish.

'My house . . .' she panted to David,
'. . . not yours.'

And she turned up the High Street
and raced off.

Goodbye, Maccaloo

SURINDER'S MOTHER STARED as they ran
in and locked the back door. 'What are
you doing?'

'Must keep Erica out,' Surinder
panted.

She led David into the sitting room,
shut the door and unbuttoned her coat.
The Maccaloo gazed up at her with
enormous, terrified eyes.

'Don't be afraid,' Surinder said.
'You're going home. Now.'

'Now?' said the Maccaloo.

'*Now?*' said David.

'Yes.'

Putting the Maccaloo down in an armchair, Surinder opened her mother's work cupboard and took out the bead jar. David looked baffled.

'Beads?'

'Not *beads*,' Surinder said. '*This* bead.'

She picked out the cloudy blue one and put it on the arm of the chair. 'That's what you want most from our world, Maccaloo. Your calling bead. If *you've* got it, no one can ever bring you here again.'

The Maccaloo stared at the bead, with its mouth open. Then it leapt from the chair on to Surinder's shoulder. Its arms went round her neck, and it rubbed its soft, furry face up and down her cheek.

For a second it stayed there, smiling happily. Then it leapt back to the chair and snatched up the bead.

FIZZ!!! A wisp of musty smoke curled over the chair. When it cleared, the Maccaloo had gone.

Surinder gazed at the chair. *Goodbye, Maccaloo*, she thought. She hoped it was happy, back in its cosy Delta-world, where the colours changed and people wore Bouncing Socks.

David nudged her. 'Look.'

Erica's face was pressed to the window. She was struggling to peer through the net curtains.

'What on earth . . . ?' said Surinder.

'We've got a secret, haven't we?' David grinned. 'She can't bear it.'

Surinder chuckled. 'Pity it's all over.'

'It doesn't have to be,' said David.

'What do you mean?'

'Well . . . some of those bouncing machines I designed for the Maccaloo were quite good. Why don't we build a few of them? In secret, of course.'

Surinder's eyes gleamed. 'Could we make one that's big enough for *us* to bounce?'

'Maybe.' David pulled the diagrams out of his pocket. 'Do you think we could do it with a lot of footballs?'

Surinder grinned. 'Let's have a go!' she said.